VEGETABLE

For
Mrs. Billings
class

Dong
Florian

GARDEN

Douglas Florian

Harcourt Brace Jovanovich, Publishers

San Diego   New York   London

Copyright © 1991 by Douglas Florian

Library of Congress Cataloging-in-Publication Data
Florian, Douglas.
Vegetable garden/Douglas Florian. — 1st ed.
p.   cm.
Summary: A family plants a vegetable garden and helps it grow
to a rich harvest.
ISBN 0-15-293383-2
[1. Gardening — Fiction.   2. Vegetables — Fiction.   3. Stories in
rhyme.] I. Title.
PZ8.3F66Ve   1991
[E] — dc 20   90-20620

The illustrations in this book were done in
pen and ink and watercolor on vellum paper.
The display type was set in Lithos Bold
by Thompson Type, San Diego, California.
The text type was set in Cushing Book
by TypeLink, San Diego, California.
Printed and bound by Tien Wah Press, Singapore
Production supervision by Warren Wallerstein and Michele Green
Type design by Lisa Peters

for Yonathan Lallouz

Spade, rake, hoe

Seeds in a row

Seedlings sprout

Weeding out

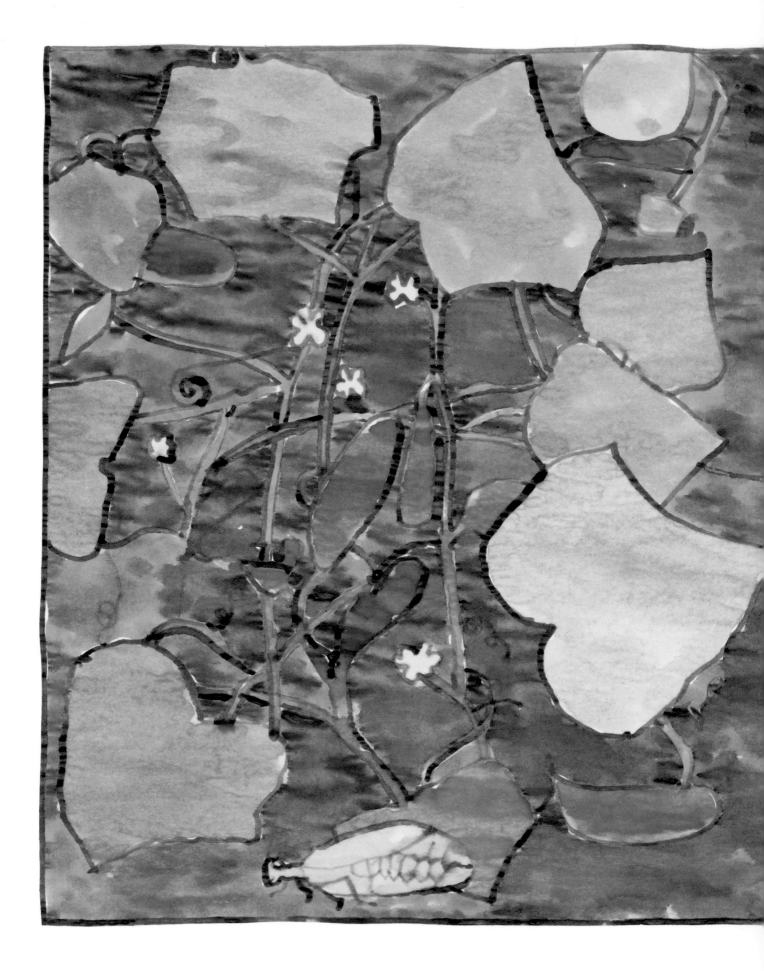

Cucumber vine

Bright sunshine

Greens and reds

Summer shower

Cauliflower

Big and round

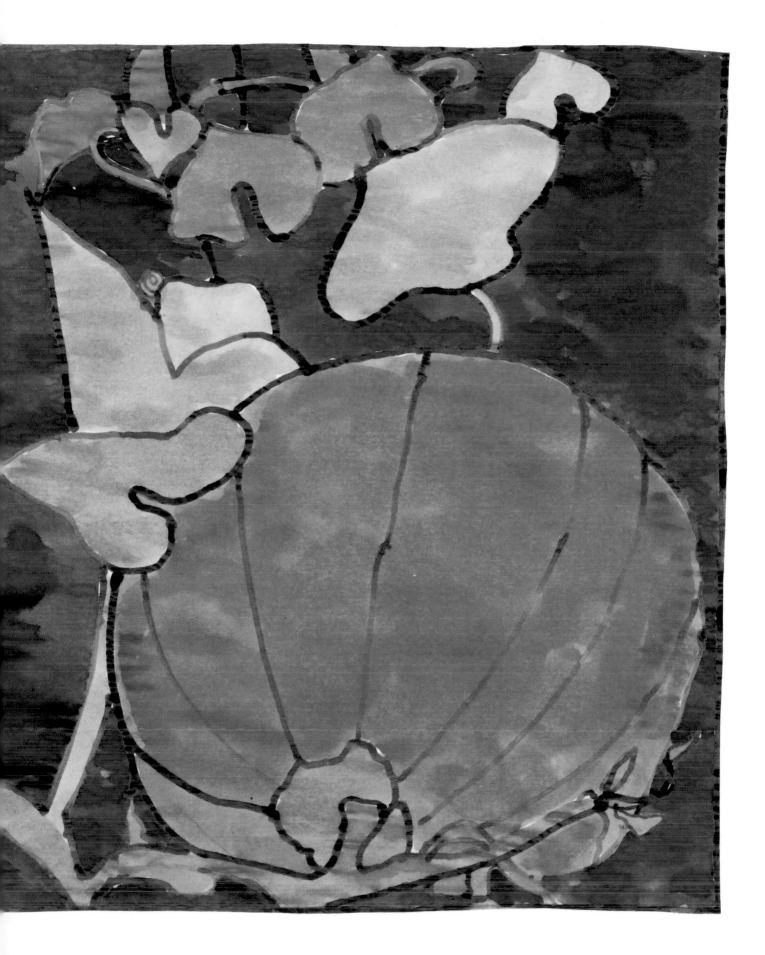

Melon mound

Pea plants climb

Harvest time